Bouncer

and the

Stream of Life

Becalm Publishing Books by Becki Balok

Wake Up! Awaken the Spirit Within and You'll Never Be the Same Again

Bouncer and the Stream of Life

Forthcoming:

Bouncer's Great Adventure

Bouncer and the Garden of Life

The Acorn and the Tree of Life

Bouncer

and the
Stream of Life

Written by Becki Balok
Illustrated by Richard F. Thomas

Becalm Publishing, Inc.
Berkley, Michigan

Copyright ©1999 by Becki Balok

First Printing – Limited Edition

Published and Distributed by:
Becalm Publishing, Inc.
P.O. Box 725378
Berkley, MI 48072
www.becalm-publishing.com

ISBN 0-9662759-1-8
Library of Congress Number: 99-095286
Printed in the U.S.A

God's will for me is perfect happiness.

—A Course in Miracles

Clouds formed in a crystal blue sky.

Soon the rain began.

A pleasant, warm rain full of small, ordinary drops.

Wherever they landed, they splashed.

One drop didn't splash.

*I*t bounced.

And no matter how many times it bounced, it just kept on bouncing.

This bouncing raindrop is Bouncer.

Oh, the places Bouncer bounced.

First, on the grass. "Ooooh, that tickles," giggled Bouncer.

Then the road. "Oh, that's smooth and fast," and Bouncer raced along the surface.

What Bouncer liked best was the space between the bounces.

That is when Bouncer flew.

Above the grass and road.

Floating. Free.

Oh, how Bouncer wanted to share the joy of bouncing with the other drops.

But, no drops would follow him.

Oh they listened politely enough. But then they would say things that seemed strange.

One said, "Perhaps it works for you Bouncer, but drops are suppose to splash. Splashing is what we do."

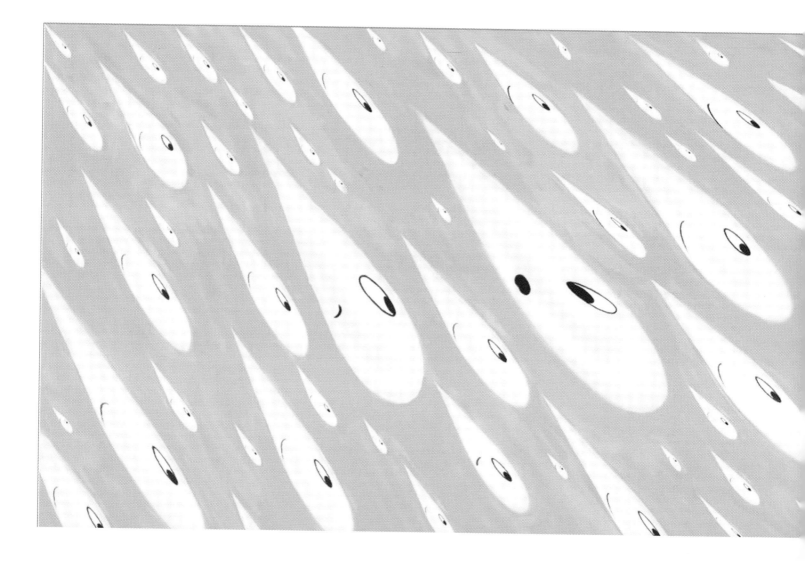

Bouncer hurriedly tried to explain, "No, no, no—don't you see, if it works for me, it'll work for you too."

Another said, "I don't deserve to bounce."

Bouncer replied, "You don't have to earn bouncing. Just try it."

Bouncer sadly realized the other drops would never bounce.

Not because they couldn't.

But because they didn't believe they could.

"I'm not like the other drops," Bouncer thought.

And Bouncer bounced.

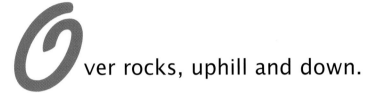ver rocks, uphill and down.

Near flowers, past ants.

The rain continued and Bouncer tried again to talk to the other drops.

One said, "Who do you think you are?"

"Why, I'm a drop, just like you," replied a confused Bouncer.

"Oh, no you're not! If you were like me you'd just splash," replied the drop angrily.

"But," Bouncer asked, "What good is splashing?"

"WHAT GOOD IS SPLASHING? WHAT GOOD IS SPLASHING?" the drop shouted.

"Splashing is as good as it gets. Drops splash. That's the way it is, always has been, always will be."

Bouncer asked bravely, "Why?"

The drop didn't answer, it just splashed.

nd Bouncer bounced.

Soon the sun began to shine. Bouncer liked the warmth.

The sun made Bouncer feel all bubbly inside.

Feeling bubbly made Bounce giggle and smile.

Bouncer noticed when he giggled and smiled he felt very happy.

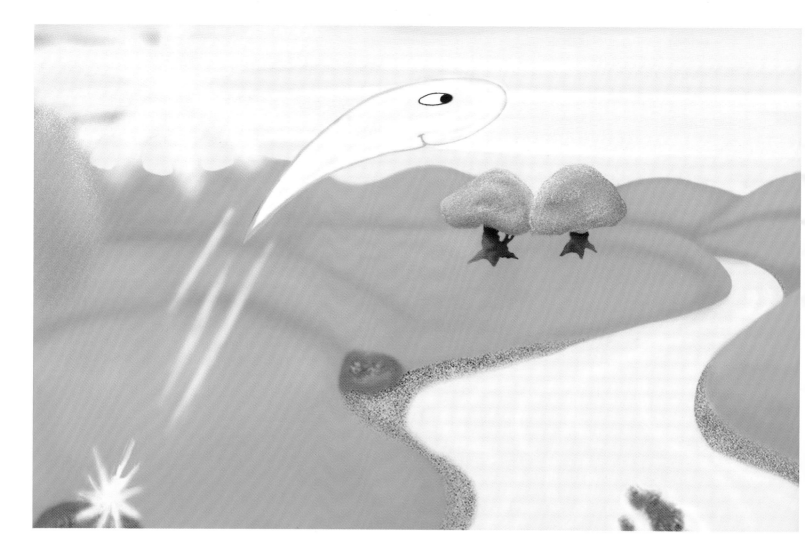

*H*e also noticed if he thought about bouncing, he bounced higher.

And when he thought about rolling, he rolled farther.

"Hmmm," Bouncer thought, "this seems very important. I wish I could find someone to help me understand it."

Just as Bouncer thought that, he found himself at a Stream.

*H*e didn't know it, of course, Bouncer had never seen a Stream before.

He wondered if it was a bunch of drops that splashed together.

Bouncer gazed at the water.

Another drop bounced out of the Stream and sat right next to him.

"Hi!"

"Oh, my goodness," said a very surprised Bouncer, "can you bounce too?"

"Of course! I'm Jumper."

"I'm very happy to meet you Jumper," Bouncer said.

"I was beginning to think I was the only bouncing drop."

"We've been waiting for you, Bouncer."

"For me . . . me?"

"Yes," said Jumper with a warm smile, "for you."

"You see," continued Jumper, "without you the Stream doesn't have enough bounce. You make it complete."

Bouncer asked, feeling a bit better now, "What's a Stream?"

"My, my, my." Jumper giggled, "You are new to this, aren't you?"

Bouncer nodded.

"We are the Stream. On the surface, we look like ordinary raindrops. But as you've discovered, Bouncer, we are more than just a bit of wet."

"We think," said Jumper, "and whatever we think about we create."

"I know," said Bouncer. "If I think about bouncing, I bounce higher. If I think about being happy, I giggle. Sometimes, I think about splashing and I leak."

"Exactly!"

"Ever since the first rain clouds formed," Jumper went on, "drops could bounce."

"The first drops knew it and decided to make some rules."

"Rules?" questioned Bouncer.

Jumper explained, "Only the biggest drops were allowed to bounce."

"But, why?" Bouncer asked.

"The big drops said bouncing had to be done perfectly. Only big drops could do it right."

"So, small drops gave up bouncing. They stopped believing they could," said Jumper.

Bouncer noticed a tear in his eye.

"But, some drops," Jumper cleared his throat, "decided to bounce anyway."

"They knew there must be more to a raindrop's life than splashing."

Jumper said proudly, "the amazing thing about bouncing is you can bounce and splash and bounce again!"

"WHAT?" exclaimed Bouncer, wondering if he had dozed off and dreamt those last words.

"You just saw me do it."

"Can I . . . ," Bouncer said very slowly, ". . . do it too?"

"Of course you can," said a confident Jumper.

"How?"

"Look carefully at the Stream," said a calm Jumper to a very excited Bouncer.

ouncer noticed fish swimming in it. The Stream was a good home for them.

Buzzing bees made him look at the flowers near the edge of the Stream. The flowers, painted with rainbow colors, were different sizes and shapes. The Stream fed them.

Bouncer saw the Stream gently flowed under, around, over or through anything in its path. The Stream was very smart and very kind.

Bouncer thought the Stream must be the source of every good thing.

"The Stream is love," Jumper said.

Bouncer started to feel a little dizzy. "That Stream is very important."

"Bouncer," said Jumper, "you are part of the Stream."

"You are connected to the Stream and that is why you can bounce, splash, and bounce again."

Bouncer said, "If the Stream is important, and I am connected to it, I must be important, too."

Jumper smiled, "You've got it!"

Bouncer smiled a shy smile not sure of what exactly he got.

"You see," continued Jumper, "in the Stream of Life we are all connected. Together we love the earth and all living things."

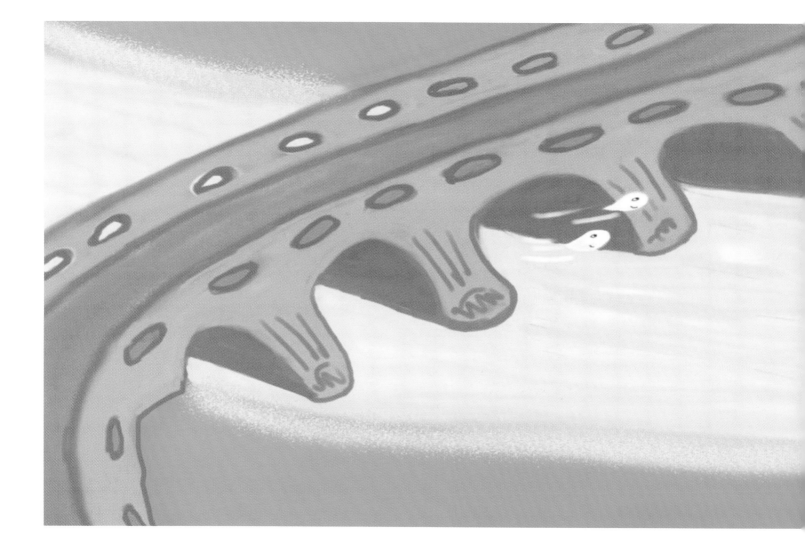

"Together we are strong. We lift each other over the rocks, around tree stumps, under bridges."

"And," continued Jumper, "no matter where you bounce, the Stream is always with you."

"In fact," Jumper exclaimed, "wherever you bounce you take the love of the Stream with you."

"That makes me sound very special," said Bouncer proudly.

"You are special!" announced Jumper.

"I'm sure glad I met you," said a relieved Bouncer.

"The other drops got so angry with me for bouncing. I was afraid bouncing was bad."

"Oh, heavens no! Bouncing is good," and he gave Bouncer a squishy hug.

Bouncer had never been hugged before. After the waves slowed down, he knew he liked hugging.

*J*umper had met Bouncer at just the right time.

"Bouncer," Jumper said sadly "until the other drops bounce they won't be able to find the Stream of Life."

Bouncer knew Jumper was a very wise drop.

"Jumper," asked Bouncer, "can we help them?"

"Ah, my friend," said Jumper. "The greatest gift we have been given is the power to choose our thoughts."

Jumper knew that thinking about bouncing, splashing, and bouncing again is a choice each and every drop must make.

"There's room for all drops in the Stream of Life and every rainy day, each drop can choose," said Jumper.

ouncer thought for a moment and feeling a bit forgetful asked, "Choose what?"

Jumper smiled a great big smile and exclaimed, "Choose to be connected to the Stream or splash."

"I know what I choose!" said a confident Bouncer.

"What?" asked Jumper hopefully.

"I want to be in the Stream of Life!"

And Bouncer bounced higher than ever before, gently splashed into the Stream, and moved with the flow to even greater bounces and splashes yet to come.

About the Author

A Michigan resident, Becki Balok, is a graduate of Hope College, Western Michigan University, and Wayne State University. Promoting her first book, *Wake Up!* has brought Becki to center stage as a enthusiastic public speaker and radio show guest.

About the Illustrator

Richard F. Thomas, who poignantly captured the heart and soul of Bouncer, lives in Gainesville, Florida.

Becalm Publishing Order Form

Send _____ copies of:
Bouncer and the Stream of Life. $9.95 (ISBN: 0-9662759-1-8)

Send _____ copies of:
Wake Up! $12.95 (ISBN: 0-9662759-0-X)

Michigan Residents add 6% (x.06) Sales Tax.
Shipping: $3.00 for first book, $1.00 for each additional. Allow 2 weeks.

Ship To Address:

Name: _____

Street: _____

City: _____

State:_____ Zip Code: _____

☐ **Check Enclosed for $**_____ (payable to Becalm Publishing, Inc.)

☐ **Charge $**_____**to my** ☐ **Visa or** ☐ **Mastercard** **Exp. Date Required**

Mo.	Yr.

Send Order Form to:

Becalm Publishing, Inc.
P.O. Box 725378
Berkley, MI 48072
Toll-Free: 1-877-7BE-CALM
Fax: (248)-288-6105